To Niélé
To the Debelle family
To the Traoré family
To Ségou and its river
M.T.

Reycraft Books
55 Fifth Avenue
New York, NY 10003

Reycraftbooks.com

Reycraft Books is a trade imprint and trademark of Newmark Learning, LLC.

© Éditions Cépages, 2018
www.editionscepages.fr
Translation rights arranged through Syllabes Agency, France
English translation in the United States ©2021 Reycraft Books

Educators and Librarians: Our books may be purchased in bulk for promotional, educational, or business use. Please contact sales@reycraftbooks.com.

This is a work of fiction. Names, characters, places, dialogue, and incidents described either are the product of the author's imagination or are used fictitiously. Any resemblance to actual persons, living or dead, is entirely coincidental.

Library of Congress Control Number: 2020925466

ISBN: 978-1-4788-7378-5

Printed in Dongguan, China. 8557/0221/17683

10 9 8 7 6 5 4 3 2 1

First Edition Hardcover published by Reycraft Books 2021

Reycraft Books and Newmark Learning, LLC, support diversity and the First Amendment, and celebrate the right to read.

Paratou, the Umbrella

Marion Traoré

REYCRAFT
BOOKS

In a small village lives Sékou, the oldest son of the village chief. Several times a week after school, he sells peanuts on the roadside. Over the past few months, he has collected a small sum of money. This Saturday he decides to go with his father to the nearest market to spend it.

Once the shopping is over, his friends spot him returning by motorcycle. He sits behind his dad holding a rainbow-colored object. It's a big umbrella that he has bargained for with a city merchant. But you should know, it never rains during this season so almost no one buys umbrellas.

Sékou jumps off the motorcycle and makes an announcement to the villagers.

"Hear ye, hear ye! Here is Paratou, the Umbrella. It's a beautiful object that everyone can use. There is just one rule: you must bring it back in good condition and leave it next to my father's hut every evening."

Since that day, the umbrella has not rested! On clear days, when the sun beats down, the mothers take the umbrella to hide in its shadow with their newborns.

On the roadside, it transforms into a "pee-shack" for bus travelers. They are happy. And it's a new opportunity for the village kids to earn some pocket money.

When the elephants come to the watering place on the river near the village, Paratou is quite helpful. Fishermen use it to protect themselves from the elephants' powerful water spray.

When it rains heavily, adults find shelter under the umbrella while children enjoy the outdoor shower.

The umbrella is used in every hide-and-seek game.
It's a hiding place for little Awa. But she is found quickly.
Can you see her? What about her other friends?

When his back hurts, Demba, the oldest man in the village, walks with the help of this multicolored companion. Abou, his grandson, is relieved, as it used to be his job to support his grandfather while walking.

The umbrella also serves as a weather reporter. If it turns inside out from a strong wind, it means rain will soon arrive in the village. Everyone gets alarmed. Maybe thunder and lightning are on the way, too?

During mango season, children use it on top of their poles. It helps them pick the mangos that are hidden in the treetops. Now they can get the sweetest and juiciest fruit.

Paratou goes to school, as well. The teacher uses it to teach the colors to her students.

Do you know them?

On Thursdays and Sundays—wedding days—it changes into a colorful sunshade for the newlyweds. The wedding procession can be seen from far away, and the guests holding the umbrella change regularly to relieve their arms.

It gets used for so many years that, despite all the care users took to keep it in good condition, the beautiful umbrella ends up broken and left at the door of Sékou's hut. He has now become the village chief.

One day, his son Boubacar finds the old umbrella and decides to buy a new gift for the villagers. He earns enough coins on the roadside and sets off for the market to spend them.

His friends see him returning with a big smile and an object in his hands. The young boy makes an announcement to the villagers.

"Hear ye, hear ye! Here is a beautiful object that everyone can use. There is just one rule: you must bring it back in good condition and leave it next to my father's hut every evening."

What object did he get for the villagers?
What can they do with it?

Box

Watering can

Hammock

Jump rope

Trash can

Rolling pin

Diving mask

Travel pillow

Kerosene lamp